Billy the Kid Goes Wild

You can read more stories about
the animals from Potter's Barn
by collecting the rest of the series.

For a complete list, look at
the back of the book.

Billy the Kid Goes Wild

Francesca Simon

Illustrated by Emily Bolam

Orion
Children's Books

Billy the Kid Goes Wild first appeared in *Moo Baa Baa Quack,*
first published in Great Britain in 1997
by Orion Children's Books
This edition first published in Great Britain in 2011
by Orion Children's Books
a division of the Orion Publishing Group Ltd
Orion House
5 Upper St Martin's Lane
London WC2H 9EA
An Hachette UK Company

1 3 5 7 9 10 8 6 4 2

ISBN 978 1 4440 0197 6

Printed in China

The Orion Publishing Group's policy is to use papers that are natural,
renewable and recyclable products made from wood grown in sustainable forests.
The logging and manufacturing processes are expected to conform
to the environmental regulations of the country of origin.

For Kate Christer

Hello from everyone

Father Goat

Bleat

Billy the Kid

at Potter's Barn!

Mother Sheep

Baaaaa

Tilly and Tam
the lambs

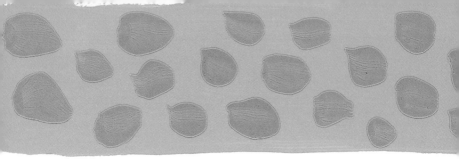

Mother Duck

Quack
Quack

Five Ducklings

Neigh

Trot the horse

Honk Honk

Gabby Goose

Woof

Buster the dog

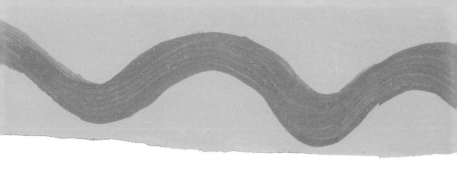

Moooo

Daffodil the cow

Rosie the calf

Oink oink

Belle the pig

Cock-a-doodle-doo!

Red Rooster

Squeaky the cat

Miaow

Henny-Penny

Cluck Cluck

The chicks

Cheep Cheep

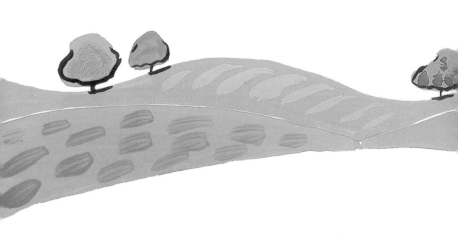

Welcome to Potter's Barn!

The sun always shines and the fun
never stops at Potter's Barn Farm.
Join the animals on their adventures
as they sing, stomp, make cakes,
get lost, run off, and go wild.

Billy the Kid
had big plans.

When he had
finished
munching the
blankets…

…he was going
to gobble some
tasty paper bags
he'd seen blowing
about in Silver
Meadow.

Then he wanted
to visit Muddy
Pond…

…watch
the fish…

...and nibble some
thorny bushes.

Then he was
off to Gabby
Goose's
birthday party.

So you can imagine
how Billy felt when
his father interrupted.

"Naptime,"
said Father Goat.

"Oh no,"
said Billy.

"Oh yes," said his father.
"If you don't nap you'll be
too tired for Gabby's party."

"No I won't," said Billy.
"Yes you will," said Father Goat.
"But I'm not tired," said Billy.

Trot poked his head
over the stable door.

"I'll help Billy feel sleepy," said Trot.
"Come on, Billy, I'll race you across
Butterfly Field."

Off they galloped.
"I won," shouted Billy the Kid.
"Race you back."

So Trot and Billy zoomed
back to the stable.

"Again!" shouted Billy.
Back and forth, back
and forth they ran.

At last Trot stood panting.
"Let's race to Far Away Field,"
said Billy.

"If you don't mind, Billy, I think
I'll just rest for a moment,"
said Trot, yawning.

He closed his eyes
and fell asleep.

"Naptime,"
said Father Goat.

"But I'm **not tired**,"
said Billy the Kid.

Squeaky the cat scampered over.
"I'll help Billy feel sleepy,"
said Squeaky.

"Come on, Billy, let's do somersaults
all the way to Muddy Pond.
Last one there is a ninny."

Off they somersaulted.

"I won," shouted Billy.
"Let's race again."

Head over heels they rolled.

At last Squeaky stood panting.

"Let's hop backwards to
the haystack now," said Billy.

"If you don't mind, Billy,"
said Squeaky, yawning,
"I think I'll just lie down
for a moment."

She closed her eyes
and fell asleep.

"Naptime,"
said Father Goat.

"But I'm still
not tired,"
said Billy.

Buster the dog and
Rosie the calf strolled by.

"We'll help Billy feel sleepy,"
said Buster. "Come on, Billy, let's
see who can bellow the loudest."

"Ruff Ruff Ruff"

"Mooooooooo"

"Maaaaaaaaaa"

Back and forth across the farmyard
they hullabalooed, louder and louder,
barking, mooing, and bleating.

At last Buster and Rosie
stood panting.

"That was fantastic," said Billy
the Kid. "Let's go and play
with Tam and Tilly now."

"If you don't mind,
Billy, I'll just lie down for a
moment," said Buster, yawning.
"Me too," said Rosie.

They closed their eyes
and fell asleep.

Just then Gabby ran out
of her shed, honking.

"Party time!"
she yelled.

"Wake up, Trot!"

"Wake up, Squeaky!"

"Wake up, Buster!"

"Wake up, Rosie!"
shouted Billy.

"It's party time."

Everyone had a lovely time at Gabby's party. They played musical statues, pass the parcel, and pin the hat on the farmer.

Then everyone ate lots and lots of
hay and corn and oats.

Well, almost everyone.

Bleat bleat
follow me

Did you enjoy
Billy the Kid's story?
Can you remember the
things that happened?

What's the second thing Billy the
Kid wants to do with his day?

What is Billy is excited about?

Why does Billy say he doesn't want to take a nap?

What does Trot the horse suggest
might make Billy sleepy?

Who is the second animal to try
and help Billy feel sleepy?

What does Squeaky reply when Billy says they should hop backwards to the haystack?

How do Buster the dog and Rosie the calf try to help Billy feel sleepy?

What sorts of games does everyone play at Gabby's party?

For more farmyard fun with the animals at Potter's Barn, look out for the other books in the series.

Where Are My Lambs?

Runaway Duckling

Barnyard Hullabaloo

Mish Mash Hash

Chicks Just
Want to
Have Fun

Moo Baa
Baa Quack